Cold-Forge

Cold-Forged Flame

ALSO BY MARIE BRENNAN

Cold-Forged Flame
Lightning in the Blood (forthcoming)

THE LADY TRENT MEMOIRS
A Natural History of Dragons
The Tropic of Serpents
Voyage of the Basilisk
In the Labyrinth of the Drakes

DEEDS OF MEN
Midnight Never Come
In Ashes Lie
A Star Shall Fall
With Fate Conspire

Warrior
Witch

MARIE BRENNAN

COLD-FORGED FLAME

A TOM DOHERTY ASSOCIATES BOOK

NEW YORK

COLD-FORGED FLAME

Copyright © 2016 by Bryn Neuenschwander

Cover illustration by Sam Weber
Cover design by Christine Foltzer

Edited by Miriam Weinberg

A Tor.com Book
Published by Tom Doherty Associates, LLC
175 Fifth Avenue
New York, NY 10010

www.tor.com

Tor® is a registered trademark of Tom Doherty Associates, LLC.

ISBN 978-0-7653-9138-4 (ebook)
ISBN 978-0-7653-9139-1 (trade paperback)

First Edition: September 2016

Cold-Forged Flame

Cold Forged Flame

The sound of the horn pierces the apeiron, shattering the stillness of that realm. Its clarion call creates ripples, substance, something more. It is a summons, a command. There is will. There is need.

And so, in reply, there is a woman.

~

She comes into existence atop a flat, rough slab of stone. In the first few instants, as the sound of the horn fades, that stone consumes all her attention: its pitted, weathered surface, shedding grit against her knuckles where her fist is braced. It is ancient, that stone, and full of memory.

As she herself is not.

She lifts her head to find she is not alone. Nine people stand in a loose arc in front of where she kneels, six men, three women, with torches all around throwing their features into shifting, untrustworthy relief. Pale, all of them, much paler than her. The torchlight lends their skin a false warmth, brightens their hair to gold or fire's orange. Every last one of them, she thinks, is holding their breath. Watching her.

On the ground before her lies the corpse of a bull, its throat neatly slit. Some of the blood fills a silver bowl set at the foot of the stone, while the rest soaks quietly into the grass. At the sight of it, her muscles tense abruptly, as if lightning has shot through her veins.

They're still watching her. They carry knives, the men and women alike, and when her free hand moves, it finds nothing at her own side. There should be a weapon, but there isn't. Which means these people have the advantage.

It isn't a good way to start.

She licks her lips, finds everything moves as it should. Tests her voice.

"Who the hell are you?"

The words come out like a whip-crack, breaking the quiet of the night. The man at the center of the arc straightens. He grips a curved horn in one hand, a bloodstained knife in the other; he is the one who sounded the call, the one who slit the bull's throat. Drawing in a deep breath, he gives the horn to the woman at his side and steps forward. He is older than the others, his hair and beard gray beneath the fire's false color, and the pin that holds his draped garment at his shoulder is richly worked gold. A leader of some kind. She focuses on him, almost as intensely as she had upon the stone.

In the tone of one speaking with ritual intent, he says, "I am Ectain cul Simnann, Cruais of my people, and I bind you to this task: to bring us blood from the cauldron of the Lhian."

The weight of it has been there all this time, lost beneath the sights and sounds, the scent of blood in the air. At his declaration, she feels that weight solidify around her, binding with a strength beyond any rope or chain. She is caught: has been since the first instant, with no hope of escape.

The fury of it drives her from her stillness. In one fluid motion, she rises from her crouch and leaps over the silver bowl of blood, the cooling body of the bull, to land in front of the leader. He has a knife and she doesn't, but it doesn't matter: at first because she's determined to kill him anyway, and then because she can't. Her hand slams to a halt before she can touch him.

It doesn't stop him from lurching backward. His eyes are wide with fear, but not surprise. So. He knew she couldn't hurt him . . . but his confidence in that protection was less than absolute.

Her lips skin back in a fierce smile. "You're safe. How about the rest of them?"

"Please!" He drops to his knees, hands raised in a gesture of peace. Then he notices the bloody knife he still clutches, and lays it down hastily. "Please. We mean you no harm. We only need you to do something for us. When that's done, you will be free to go, with our blessings and our thanks—you have my word."

What good is his word, when he's a stranger to her? Ectain cul Simnann, Cruais of his people: sounds with no meaning. She knows blood; she knows knives. She doesn't know him.

She casts a cold stare across the others. They've clumped together for comfort and safety, backing up toward one of the tall stones that ring this place. None of them have laid down their knives. They won't attack her, though: they need her for something. To bring them blood from the cauldron of the Lhian—whoever or whatever that might be. So they'll be hesitant if she goes for them. She felt the easy response of her body when she leapt from the stone, how readily her muscles answered her call. She's pretty sure she could kill one, two—maybe even three—before they subdue her.

Part of her wants to do it, just for what they've done. Binding her to their will.

It won't accomplish anything, of course. That's the meaning of the lead weighing down her bones: sooner or later, she will *have* to do as this man commands, whether she kills everyone he brought with him or not. The only thing murder would accomplish would be to turn him against her—assuming he actually means what he said, about letting her go afterward. But there's a significant part of her that wants to say *fuck it* and kill them anyway.

"Please," the Cruais whispers. It draws her attention back to him, which is probably what he intended. He's arranged himself more formally now, with his hands curled into fists and set against the ground. "I could bind you not to harm them. But I don't want to. All I want is for you to bring us the blood."

What tugs at her now isn't the binding. It's curiosity. "Why do you need it? What's so special about this blood?"

He shakes his head. "It's better if I don't tell you."

Her breath huffs out in disbelief. "Right. Then let's try something else. Who, or what, is the Lhian? Where can I find this cauldron?"

A dead leaf clings to his knuckle when he lifts one hand to gesture at a young man watching from nearby. She can see a family resemblance in the wide-set eyes, the rounded cheeks that have fallen into jowls on the Cruais. "Therdiad will take you, as far as he can go."

"That isn't an answer."

"Forgive me." He sets his fist back down, bows forward until his head nearly touches the ground. She can see his arms shaking as he bends: from age or nerves, or maybe both. "I understand your frustration—"

"I don't think you do." She drops to one knee and

seizes the collar of his tunic. It's partly a test: yes, she can touch him, so long as she doesn't plan on inflicting bodily harm. But maybe he doesn't know that, because a small sound of fear escapes him when her hand closes around the fabric and jerks him up from his bow.

In a low voice, iron-hard with anger, she says, "I have *nothing*. I don't know who you are. I don't know who *I* am. I don't know where this place is, what is going on, or why the fuck you need me to do this for you, apart from guessing that you're a coward too scared to do it for himself. All I know is that apparently I have no choice: I have to do what you say. The *least* you owe me in return is some information."

He sags in her grip, not fighting. "I do this for the good of my people."

"Your people don't mean a damned thing to me."

"I know. And you have no reason to believe me. When you return, I promise I will answer your questions—all of them, as completely as I can. You are right, that I owe you that. But for now..." His mouth trembles, then steadies. "I do this for your own good as well. The less you know, the safer you will be."

A snarl builds in her throat. She asks questions, and he gives her only a paradox in return. If what he says is true, there must be a reason. But if what he says is true, then he can't *tell* her that reason—not without defeating his own purpose. Which means she's supposed to trust him.

Every instinct rebels at that thought. He's a stranger—no, worse. He's the man holding her leash. There's no basis in that for trust. And she has nothing to draw on for strength or reassurance, because inside her there's a gaping void, an abyss where *everything* should be: memory, understanding, knowledge. Her sense of self. She might as well be dying of thirst in the desert, and he's holding a skin of water, warning her that it's poisoned.

How the hell do I even know what a desert is?

That question loosens her grip. The Cruais scrambles out of range, standing once more. He reaches below the collar of his tunic and draws out a vial on a cord, which he offers to her with an unsteady hand. But when he speaks, his voice is stronger. "Please. I swear to you on my sister's heart that I will give you everything when you return. An explanation. Your freedom. Any gifts of gold or supply that we can give you. But you must go."

When he says that, the hook buried in her spirit tugs in response. Yes: she has to go. But she also has to come back.

He doesn't flinch when she snatches the vial from his hand, like a cat taking its prey. When she fixes her gaze on him, though, he shivers. She takes black satisfaction in that. "If you don't make good on your promise," she says, "then I swear on my own blood: you will pay for it."

The lightning in her body sparks in response.

~

Therdiad takes her: the Cruais's grandson, she thinks. He's dressed much like the old man, although the pin on his shoulder is less elegantly worked. She doesn't ask. What does it matter, who takes her on this journey? She's just as fucked regardless.

The torchlight fades behind them, but she can still see it for a long distance in this flat, grassy terrain. The sky above is clear and brilliant with stars, no moon to outshine them. She doesn't feel much like talking to Therdiad: they walk in silence, while the stars move slowly overhead.

She loses track of how long they're out there, settling into the comfortable rhythm of walking. It comes as an unwelcome surprise when she hears a steady, rushing pulse up ahead, breaking the quiet. Water. Waves. *The sea,* she thinks. The word brings an image to mind, though she can't remember ever having seen it.

There are more lights, too, a dim glow off to the left. "Is that a town?" she asks.

Therdiad casts a glance that way, then promptly veers right. Away from the lights. "That isn't where we're going."

"How am I to know?" she says dryly, following. "It isn't like you've given me a map."

"It won't be much farther," Therdiad says. "We're looking for a rowboat."

"Your rowboat? Or will any rowboat do? I wonder . . . could be that's your home back there, and you don't want me to see it. Or could be you're on somebody else's land here, and you're afraid of getting caught." His shoulders twitch at the second suggestion, and she grins at his back, feral. "I see. So we're stealing a rowboat from the good people of that place."

Therdiad pauses long enough to give her what she suspects is his best glare. It doesn't leave much of a mark. "I'm not a thief. The boat is ours. We left it there last night, before we went to the ring of stones."

Nine people wouldn't fit in any boat Therdiad could row on his own. Carrying a boat overland would be inconvenient; that suggests they came by water, and there's a second boat somewhere, which brought the rest of the group here. She calculates this reflexively, even though it doesn't lead her anywhere useful: if she wants to escape, it would be easier to wait until Therdiad finds the boat, then club him over the head and take the boat for her own. Or just run for that town. She might get at least a little distance away, before the hook buried in her gut drags her back to her path.

Running would be a waste of time, and not one she feels like indulging in. But she still thinks about these things, as if it's habit.

They find the boat pulled up above the tide line in a small inlet, where the tiny slope gives it all the cover to be had in this flat terrain. It's a narrow sliver, wooden-ribbed, covered in cured hide. Much too small for nine people; four would be cramped. She wonders where the other boat is.

Therdiad puts his hand on the edge and says, "Help me?" for all the world as if they're working together. She snorts and takes the other side.

At least he doesn't ask her to row. He arranges the oars and gets them out past the breakers with the skill of someone who's done this a lot, then settles into a comfortable rhythm, like she did on the walk here. "I hope your strength holds out," she says, "because I don't remember the last time I rowed."

The sarcasm misses him completely. "It isn't far," he says. "The island is in the middle of the bay."

So it's a bay they're in, not the open sea. Probably too wide for her to swim, though—especially since she has no idea whether she knows how to swim.

A thin mist rises as he rows. She can see the moon just above the horizon now, a sharp crescent. Waning, she thinks—which means it isn't long until dawn. Another thing she knows, as if she's been awake on count-less nights she can't recall.

"Thank you," Therdiad says without warning.

She can't help raising an eyebrow. "For . . ."

"Doing this. It's very—"

He stops, and she regards him with an ironic eye. "Brave of me?"

Therdiad ducks his chin. "I was going to say kind."

But it isn't, and they both know it. There can be no kindness without choice. No courage, either. She hasn't even been kind in how she's dealt with the situation.

It says something about Therdiad, though, that he wanted to thank her anyway.

He continues rowing. There's nothing to see but the dark, low waves, and the two of them in the boat. She put the vial around her neck when they started walking; now she lifts it and examines it in the faint light of the moon. The shaft, she thinks, is made of bone, hollowed out. Human or animal? She can't tell. The stopper is more bone, carved to fit tightly, with a hole in the top where the leather cord is threaded through. The entire thing is barely the size of her finger; it won't hold much blood. Whatever they need it for, they don't need a lot.

She tucks the vial away inside the neck of her shirt and looks around for something else to occupy herself. Her gaze falls on a pistol laid on the bench at Therdiad's side.

He catches her looking. He stiffens and the rhythm of his rowing falters, as if he's fighting the urge to drop his oars and move the gun out of her reach.

"Don't worry," she says, mouth quirking. "I'm not going to shoot you."

He doesn't look reassured. After the threats she made to the Cruais, it's no surprise.

She shrugs and leans back, bracing her hands against the stern of the boat and stretching her legs out, as if at leisure. "You're taking me where I have to go, aren't you? I shoot you, I just end up having to row myself there. Not worth the trouble."

"Very comforting," he mutters, but a hint of a grin tightens the corner of his mouth. His rowing gets stronger again.

After a few more strokes, she lets herself study the gun again, openly this time. "I'm just wondering how I recognize that thing. I know it's a pistol; I know you hold one end and point the other at somebody you want to kill, and then you pull the trigger to lower the match and a bullet comes out at high speed—though I'd have to light the match first. I'm pretty sure I could load it if I tried." That isn't what her hands itch for, though. She isn't sure what is. "I even think I know that what you have there is an antique—there are better guns out there than matchlocks. How can I know all that, when I don't remember anything from before I opened my eyes on that slab?"

Therdiad doesn't answer. But from the way he bends his effort to the task of rowing, she knows he *has* answers, and is holding them back. The Cruais should have sent someone else. Someone more ignorant, or a better liar.

She asks, voice flat, "Did I even exist before that moment?"

"No," Therdiad says. Then: "Yes."

He drops the oars. They rattle in their locks, heavy and wet, but there's a collar that will keep them from sliding all the way out and being lost in the waves. She's paying attention to that, but he isn't, leaning forward with his elbows on his knees and his hands clasped tight.

"Don't," he says, full of intensity. "Don't try to remember. You can if you try—maybe—but it really is better for you if you don't."

"Why?" She resists the urge to grab him by the shoulders. That won't work this time; it will only make him stop talking. "Is there something dangerous in my memories?"

He shakes his head. "It isn't that. I mean, maybe—I don't know what you would remember. But that isn't why I'm warning you. The more you remember . . . the more you might end up losing."

It puts a core of ice in her gut. She wants to ask him

to explain, but he's already pulling back, regretting having said that much. Even so— "How the ever-loving *hell* do your people expect me to succeed at this, if I'm supposed to go through it blind?"

"You'll succeed." He picks up the oars again, resumes rowing. "That's why we brought you here."

~

The mist grows thicker. And then, so suddenly she's not sure she believes it was there a heartbeat ago, there is an island.

It looks nothing like the gentle shore they left behind. Here, stone cliffs spike upward, black shadows in what little light is available; the beach is a narrow, rocky strip crouched at their base. The place draws her eye, in much the same way the rock beneath her did when everything began. Back then it was because everything felt new, fresh: sound, after long silence; light, after an eternity in darkness. Here . . . the island just feels different. As if it doesn't quite fit into the waters around it.

"There's a mountain near the center of the island," Therdiad says, "and a cave somewhere in it. That's where you'll find the cauldron."

So she isn't traveling entirely blind. Just mostly. She studies the island as they approach, but can't see much through the mist. Should the sun have risen yet? She has no sense of the time. It seems brighter than it should be, but not like dawn. There's no glow on the horizon, either.

Therdiad stops rowing a little way out from shore. She eyes the gap between. "You can't take me the rest of the way?" The water here is preternaturally calm, waves no more than ripples a few inches high. There's no risk of damage to the boat, unless there are sharp rocks she can't see below the surface.

"Sorry," Therdiad says. "It isn't safe for me."

But it's safe for me? Of course not. She's just the one they decided to send into danger. The hook tugs and she sighs, swinging one leg over the edge of the boat.

Therdiad's voice stops her. "What you said. Calling the Cruais a coward."

When she looks back, he's biting his lip. "Others did try," he says. "Not the Cruais, it's true. But that's because others volunteered. Men and women who were eager to help."

If any of them had succeeded, she wouldn't be here. "How many of them lived to come home?"

He's clearly regretting having said anything. Therdiad picks at a rough spot on his palm and says, "One."

She could ask how many tried . . . but what would be the point? "That's the most inspiring farewell speech I can remember," she says, and drops into the cold water.

~

By the time she makes it to shore, Therdiad is already a vague shadow in the distance, the sound of his oars muffled by the fog. It occurs to her, far too late, to wonder how she's supposed to get off the island once she obtains this blood they've sent her for.

That unanswered question doesn't bother her as much as it should. Even though she knows she's been forced into this—even though she figures she's going to die—she's in a better mood than she was at first. It's obscurely satisfying, knowing there's a mountain somewhere with a cave, a cauldron in that cave, blood in that cauldron, and she will find them. Her feet are itching to get started.

And itching in a literal sense, from the salt water and grit. She finds a stone big enough to sit on and pulls off her boots, letting her feet dry while she takes a look around.

There isn't much to see yet, not with the light still so dim. On one side, water and mist; on the other, cliffs; in between lies this rocky beach. Rivulets of water trail off the cliffs in various spots, which prove to be fresh when she tastes them. She uses them to rinse the salt from her skin, washing out the inside of her boots. The leather will be wet for a long time, but there's no helping that.

She hasn't paid much attention to her own clothing before now. It's simple stuff: black boots, black breeches made of sturdy canvas, and a black shirt without sleeves or collar. Nothing like what the Cruais's people wore, with their tunics and drapes of brightly patterned wool. She doesn't think they put these clothes on her; the fabric feels well-worn and comfortable, the boots already shaped to her feet. Which means . . . what? That she had them before? *Whenever "before" was.*

The stones of the beach are sharp enough under her feet that she puts the boots back on, even though they're still damp, and begins her search. The cliffs, she thinks, can be climbed—but it won't be easy, and she doesn't much relish the thought of shredding her hands on them. She heads off in a clockwise direction, looking for a gully or the end of the cliffs, some place where they give way to easier terrain.

She walks for long enough to draw two conclusions. First, while the sun may be rising somewhere, it isn't here—and may never be. And second, there is no end to the cliffs.

"You knew it wouldn't be easy," she mutters to herself, giving the cliffs a baleful look. She isn't positive she's made a full circuit of the island yet, because she didn't think to mark her starting point. *Assuming that would have done any good.* But she's seen enough to be pretty sure there's no point in continuing to search. It's the cliffs, or nothing.

They're going to tear her hands bloody if she doesn't find some way to protect herself. She contemplates her shirt, then shakes her head. Wrapping her hands in that would require her to find or break a rock to cut with, and enough fabric to really protect her hands would leave her without much of a shirt to wear.

The only other thing out here is seaweed. Fortunately, there's plenty of that, and it comes in convenient strips. She finds some above the current waterline, still wet enough to be supple—nothing here is dry, really—but not too slick. It tastes of brine when she uses her teeth to pull the knots closed. She eyes the wrappings dubiously, curling her hands into experimental fists. The seaweed will play merry hell with her grip.

But she doesn't have anything better, and so she approaches the cliff and looks for her first handhold.

She's barely off the ground when she decides the wrappings were a terrible idea. She couldn't pull the strips tight enough to keep them from sliding, and now they shift every time her weight moves. When she grips harder to compensate, the stone cuts into the soft mass, and pretty soon she's got bits of seaweed dangling from her palms like thick, salty hair. She tries to sweep them under her hand the next time she reaches for a hold, just to get as much use out of the padding as she can before it's reduced to mere decoration: that turns out to be a mistake. Her grip fails, and she falls.

The good news is that she hasn't gotten very high. The bad news is that she's high enough for landing to hurt.

The stones of the beach roll out from under her feet as she hits, dumping her onto her ass. She bites her tongue when her head snaps back, and tastes a hint of blood. Once she's got her breath back, she spits to one side and tears what remains of the seaweed off her hands. *Fuck. That went even worse than you expected.*

Her fall teaches her one thing, at least. The Cruais's command may drive her onward . . . but it doesn't protect her from failure. If she makes a bad decision, gets herself killed, that binding will not save her.

It's anger as much as the compulsion that sends her back to her feet. Wiping her hands on her shirt, she glares at the cliff. "Let's try this again."

This time the going isn't that bad—at first. The mist and rivulets of water render the stone slippery, but without the seaweed making things worse, she can cope. The cliff face is broken enough to provide her with a variety of handholds. She moves crabwise up a diagonal, following a striation in the rock. But the jagged stones that provide her with edges to grip also tear at her skin just like she imagined, no matter how carefully she settles her fingers. Her feet can't take as much of her weight as she'd like; the boots are clumsy, and if she descends and takes them off, she'll be walking on bleeding feet the rest of the way. She'd rather sacrifice her hands.

The last few lengths are the worst, because by then her grip is slick with blood. One failure and she'll fall again, this time from a much higher point. She laughs bitterly at a tiny fern growing in front of her eyes. "If I'm going to fall, then I damn well hope I'm high enough to die when I hit the ground. None of this bullshit about lying there with broken legs until I die of exposure."

The fern doesn't respond. She clenches her teeth and climbs on, until she reaches the top.

Up there, the ground is smooth and padded with moss. She rolls onto her back, breathing hard, every muscle in her body going limp. Her hands ache steadily, pain radiating up her arms. The moss might work as a bandage, if she tears thin strips off her shirt to bind the pads in place. She didn't think to bring a rock to cut the fabric, though.

When her breath has steadied, she sits up and finds that where her hands had been, the moss is now red with blood. Genuinely *red*: the sky above her is clear, the moon's crescent sliver near the horizon—the wrong horizon, she thinks—but even in that monochrome light, the stain is vivid with color. And when she touches it, that color comes up in her fingers: a long strip of red cloth.

She stares at it, unblinking. The fabric is long and thin, and not raw; someone has stitched it into a sash. It wasn't there when she collapsed.

A swift glance around reveals no one. Not that anybody could have put that under her hands without her noticing—but she has to look anyway.

The sensible thing to do would be to take a stone from top of the cliffs and use it to cut the sash up for bandages. There are two problems with that, though. The first is that the cliffs are gone: to her left, the ground now descends in an easy series of moss-covered boulders to the shore not far below.

The second is that she doesn't want to destroy her sash. She catches herself thinking of it that way: not *the* sash, but *her* sash. Which, she supposes, is only fair. If this is what her blood turned into, then it belongs to her.

She rises to her feet, still holding the fabric in her bloody hands. The feeling of lightning is back, dancing along her veins. Without ever making a conscious decision, she finds herself tying the sash around her waist, leaving the ends to hang free. Her hands form the knot as if they've done this before, countless times, and for a moment there's a flicker: an ephemeral breath of memory, a sense that this is how she always dresses, except it's incomplete. She feels the absence of long sleeves, leather cuffs around her wrists, a weight at her hip.

Her breath comes faster. *It's safer if you don't remember.*

So Therdiad claims, and the Cruais. But can she believe them?

It's too late now, regardless; the flicker is gone. All she knows is that the sash feels right—as much as anything can feel right on this island, where cliffs vanish while her back is turned and the moon will never set.

She's beginning to understand why only one of the Cruais's people survived.

~

From here she can see the mountain. It's hard to judge distance—and if the cliffs are anything to go by, she can't assume the mountain will stay put. There's a forest in the way, too, and she knows that once she gets under its branches, keeping oriented won't be easy. No point looking for a path, though. The forest isn't likely to be any more helpful than the cliffs were.

She sets off across the soft, spongy ground, with an easy, regular stride that feels like she's used to walking long distances. At least the forest doesn't run away: soon enough she passes underneath the first branches, ducking when they're low enough to clip her in the head.

Even in their shadow, there's more light than there should be, and before long she has the creeping feeling that the forest is watching her. Now that she knows the land can change, she can't take anything for granted. This is more than just a landscape; it's a test, one that's either self-aware or controlled by someone else. Presumably the Lhian—unless the island itself is the Lhian. But no amount of guessing will tell her what the Lhian wants. *Apart from making life difficult for visitors.*

It's hard going, though at least the forest doesn't make her bleed. The ground here is uneven, and choked with underbrush, growing more thickly than she thinks it should when the tree canopy is so dense. Low vines tangle her feet; fallen, half-rotted branches crack under her weight and throw her off balance. Without anything better to guide her, she seeks out the slopes, on the principle that she'll have to go uphill eventually if she wants to climb the mountain, and she might as well start now. Her feet chafe inside her damp boots, but she doesn't bother looking to see if she has blisters. Whether she does or not, she has to keep walking.

She doesn't tire.

Her pulse beats strongly and her breath comes fast, but her energy doesn't flag. It's as if time doesn't exist here. There's no real way to tell if she's making progress; she's definitely gone a long distance, but may or may not be any closer to her goal. After a while it becomes strange, dreamlike: she might be going in circles, for all she can tell, caught in an endless loop, passing the same trees and stones over and over and over again.

No. The Lhian can put obstacles in her path—cliffs, trackless forests—and they might mislead or even kill her, but they can't stop her from moving forward. The certainty of that is so disorienting that she halts, putting one raw hand on the trunk of a tree, holding on to it as if it's the only thing keeping her from floating away.

How do I know these things?

She isn't sure she wants the answer to that question.

Part of her does. That part wants to spit in the face of Therdiad and the Cruais, tell them where they can shove their insistence that she's better off ignorant. So what if knowing will make things worse? It isn't like her current state is anything to treasure. And at least knowing would fill this void inside her, the feeling that she has somehow lost the core of her soul. Even if it turns out that what she's lost isn't anything she wants back.

The other part of her is getting all too creative, imagining what might happen if she remembers. At least this, right now, is something she can endure. What if the alternative turns out to be too much?

"Fuck that," she mutters, digging her bloody fingers into the rough bark of the tree. Then she lifts her head and addresses the forest. "And fuck you, too, Lhian. Whoever you are. Whatever you are. For all I know, you're messing with my head right now."

Nothing answers. She snarls and walks on.

Until the ground gives way without warning, and she goes ass over shoulders down a slope she never saw coming. Even as she's slamming into one stone after another, she thinks, *Of course you won't play fair.* Then she comes to a sprawling halt, limbs flung out in all directions across the ground.

The air is cold enough now for her breath to fog it, and she feels hoarfrost on the grass beneath her fingers. No branches block the sky above; it's patchy with clouds, and a full moon shines ice-white through the gaps, its beams slicing down like blades.

She stares up at the moon and considers laughing. The entire thing is a game, and it's rigged from the start. Why even bother playing?

Because she's bound to, with a chain she can't break.

And because the only way out is through.

When she rolls over and rises to her knees, she finds she's in a small valley. A stream trickles along its length, fringed with ice. There's no sign of the bay, but she's made a little progress toward the mountain's peak. *At this rate, it should only take me another six or seven eternities to get there.*

The thought is barely complete when she sees movement out of the corner of her eye.

What happens then is instinct. She spins to face whatever is approaching, feet braced to meet the oncoming target, and her hand coming down as if to slash. It doesn't matter that she has no weapon: this isn't a conscious action, a rational answer to the fact that something is coming toward her at speed. It's habit, soul-deep, an awareness that this is what she *should* do, what she *always* does, what it is in her nature to do.

And when her hand does comes down, a blade follows the arc.

It cuts through the thing rushing at her. She doesn't have any name for what she faces: she doesn't even have time to think about what it is. The creature is terror and threat, and it is not alone. They're all around her, coming out of nowhere, because the Lhian does not play by any decent rules. And she discovers that this is something she knows, whirling in their midst with a sabre in her hand, not sure if she'll survive but damned if she'll go down without a fight. She's done this before, other creatures, other battles, and in the distant, empty reaches of her memory she knows what it feels like to die. The thought of it doesn't particularly frighten her. If anything, death seems familiar.

But she doesn't die. The things she's fighting have the

shape of people, but they're something else—dreams gone wrong, maybe. One of them rushes at her, and she feels a faint, distant echo of shattering pain, the agony of love betrayed. When she cuts it down, another one replaces it: great works forgotten and fallen into dust. But if she ever achieved some great work, if she was ever in love, she doesn't remember it. Is this what the Cruais meant, and Therdiad? The snarling creatures can't get their claws into her because there's nothing to grab, no memory of either the good or its inevitable end. She laughs as they fall to her blade. *The only ones hurt by hope are those who believe in it.*

She almost cuts the stranger in half, too. Caught up in the battle, she doesn't know when he first appeared; she just knows that one of the things moving in the shifting moonlight is different, a real person among all the broken dreams. He's got a pair of knives, and sinks them into the back of something that used to be the steadfast loyalty of a friend, before that warmth turned cold.

The help is useful, and so she leaves him for last.

When every one of the twisted things has fallen, she turns on him. But maybe he expected that, because he drops to his knees, releasing the knives and raising his empty hands in a gesture reminiscent of the Cruais's. Her cut parts the air above his head. "Peace! I'm not one of them."

"I can see that," she snaps, blade held ready. "What are you?"

He risks a glance upward, trying to catch her gaze. "Just a man. Someone else trying to reach the cave of the Lhian."

It gives her pause. When she looks at him—sees him as a person, rather than a threat—he seems ordinary enough. Different from the Cruais's people: his skin is a shade darker than her own, his hair equally black, but loosely curled. He's wearing a leather vest instead of a tunic and draped wrap, and the prickling of his skin says he feels the cold more than she does. He speaks with an accent, too, and it makes her suddenly aware of the language she's speaking *as* a language. One of many in the world—because there is a world beyond this island, and the ring of stones where her memories begin.

But none of that makes him trustworthy. Her voice flat, she says, "You just happen to be here at the same time I am. And you just happen to come to my rescue."

"I wouldn't call it a rescue," he says, self-deprecating. "You were doing just fine. But I saw those things swarming you, and I thought it would be rude to leave you to fight them on your own."

It's a disarming answer—which only makes her more suspicious. On an island where cliffs can vanish and the moon can change phase on a whim, any help is not to be trusted. "So you acted out of the kindness of your heart?"

"Can I put my hands down?"

She considers it. Then she says, "Move back." When he does, she'll kick his knives out of reach. She can probably take him even if he's armed, but why make it any harder for herself than she has to?

Apparently he's making the same calculation, because he hesitates. "Look—I gave you the benefit of the doubt, coming to your aid. I figure, if the Lhian wants to play a trick like that, she'll send a poor damsel in distress. Not a perfectly capable swordswoman. But I'm not quite so certain that I want to make myself helpless, you understand?"

His choice of term for her makes her think of the sabre she holds, and how it came to be there. She wonders if he saw that part: how her hand closed on a shaft of moonlight, and the light became curved steel. That's twice now the island has given her something, and she still doesn't know why. She ought to throw both gifts away. Nothing so far in this endless night has led her to believe the Lhian is generous.

It's clear this man knows more about the Lhian than she does—starting with the fact that the Lhian is female. She's willing to play along for a while, to learn what she can. "Fine. You can put your hands down."

He does. Then, moving slowly, he picks up the knives

and sheathes them at his waist. Only when that is finished does he stand and extend one hand. "Aadet Temini."

It takes her a moment to realize it's his name. And that puts her in a bad position, because the last thing she wants to do is admit that she doesn't remember her own. She takes refuge in hostility. "Give me one reason I should trust you."

"We aren't in competition," he says. "I've never heard that the Lhian will only deal with one person at a time. There are stories of people coming in groups—the Surasim come to mind. There were three of them, two sisters and a brother, and the Lhian struck deals with them all. You won't lose anything by traveling with me."

"Unless you aren't what you claim to be. How do I know you aren't another test?"

He smiles wryly. "How do you know the test isn't whether you'll be courteous to a stranger who came to your aid?"

Irritatingly, he has a point. But she's achieved her goal, distracting him from introductions; he drops his hand. In return, she sheathes the sabre as best she can, sliding it under her sash and hoping the blade won't slice through the cloth at an inopportune moment. *Pity the island couldn't give me a proper scabbard, too.* Though for all she knows, that will show up later.

"You want to travel together," she says. "Why?"

He turns to regard the mountain looming overhead. "Well, we have to get up there somehow. And you may not have noticed, but this island is a treacherous place. I figure we stand a better chance if we each have someone to watch our back."

That presumes she trusts him, which she still doesn't. But trust isn't necessary. She'll watch her own back, and in the meanwhile get what use she can out of him. "I don't suppose you know exactly where the cave is?"

Aadet snorts. "I was hoping you could tell me that."

His ignorance eases the tension between her shoulder blades. If he'd given her the answer, she would have been sure this was a trap. She studies the landscape, then points off to the right. "It looks like that ridge leads a fair way up before it peters out."

He nods, but doesn't move yet. "I didn't get your name."

Damn it. Not so distracted after all. She says, "I only give my name to people I trust," and sets off for the ridge without looking back. In the privacy of her mind, she adds, *And apparently I don't trust myself.*

~

They start the climb in silence, but it doesn't last for long.

Aadet is garrulous, and as she hopes, the occasional laconic comment of her own is enough to keep him talking for a good stretch of time. "I think I've been on the island for three days," he says to her. "As near as I can tell, anyway, judging by the meals I've eaten. But every time I go to sleep, I wake up with no idea how long I've been out. It could be an hour or a month, for all I know."

He's carrying a pack, which he retrieved from where he'd left it before charging into the fray. She saw him notice her own lack of gear, but he hasn't said anything about it yet. When she considers her stomach, she feels like she *could* eat. She isn't really hungry, though. It's an advantage of a sort. She wonders if she'll start to feel sleepy any time soon.

None of these thoughts are the sort of thing she wants to share with him. "How did you get here?"

"Stole a boat," he says, which makes her think of her conversation with Therdiad. "Well, kind of. I left some money, but I don't really know how much boats are worth around here. I made the mistake of telling the people in Dunrist that I wanted to get to the Lhian's island, and after that, nobody would even talk to me, let alone help. I guess they think it's an ill omen."

"I can't imagine why," she says, not even trying to sound sincere.

Aadet shrugs. "She's not as bad as some. All the stories

say she only interferes with people who come to her island—doesn't go looking for trouble, the way others do."

"And the stories, of course, are true."

"They generally are," he says. "I mean, I'm not saying people never exaggerate, or forget details. But if it isn't in her nature to go after people, then she won't. She has to follow her own rules." He falls silent, looking troubled. "Unless she changes aspects, maybe. Who knows."

His words itch, deep in the recesses of her mind. *Of course the stories are true.* She spoke sarcastically before, but now she believes it, and doesn't know why.

She wants to encourage him to keep talking, to explain the things she can't ask about without revealing the depths of her ignorance. But before she can think of a subtle way to approach it, he adds, "I can't blame the people in Dunrist. It makes people's skin crawl, looking out over the water and seeing an island that wasn't there yesterday."

So it isn't just the cliffs that appear and disappear without warning. And it explains the secrecy: if the locals don't want any dealings with the Lhian, then no wonder the Cruais's people have to sneak about. She doesn't think they came a very long distance, though. The name of Dunrist sounds like it comes from the same language as their own names—which is different from the language she's been speaking. Aadet, on the other hand . . .

she's pretty sure he came from farther away.

Memory whispers. There are other languages in there, she thinks. But she can't imagine what good those would do her right now, so she grits her teeth and focuses on the terrain. There might be more of those creatures out there, or something worse.

"What about you?" he asks, before she can divert him with another comment. "How did you get here?"

She considers a variety of replies. Refusing to answer the question would be easiest, but she has a suspicion that if she does that too often, he'll stop talking entirely. Then her one source of information will dry up. No, better to save her refusals for important matters. "Someone else rowed me over," she says. "Left me on the beach."

"A friend?"

"Not exactly."

He pauses to wipe moisture from his brow. It might be sweat, or it might be the mist, which has thickened around them again. At least it isn't quite as cold as before. "I'd ask where you come from, but you won't tell me, will you?"

Not even if I knew the answer. She just passes him and keeps moving.

They're partway up the ridge now, not quite walking, not quite climbing. Her hands ache whenever she has to pull herself up a steep bit; the rush of the fight kept her from feeling it at the time, but her sliced palms and fingers haven't miraculously turned back into healthy skin. The blade of her sabre keeps clanging against the rocks, catching in crevices or snagging in the branches of a ragged bush. It hasn't yet cut through her sash, though, and that's something.

For a while the slope takes enough of Aadet's breath that he stops talking. She doesn't mind the challenge; it gives her something to think about, besides all her unanswered questions. When they attain the top of the ridge, the ground flattens out, giving a nice view of the landscape below. She thinks she might even see the waters of the bay, in between bands of mist, but Aadet distracts her from it. "I could be cagey too, I suppose," he says, his panting interrupting the words. "But what's the point? I don't see that it hurts me, telling you things about myself. And maybe you'll learn from my open and friendly example."

"Not bloody likely," she says, before she can think better of it.

But Aadet only grins. "I'll take that as a challenge. Mind if we rest for a moment? I could use a bite to eat."

She hesitates, but the hook in her soul doesn't drag her too forcefully onward. She shrugs and sits down on a flat bit of boulder.

Aadet slings his pack off his back and drops cross-legged to the ground. "Really, it's pure luck that I'm here," he says as he pulls out a loaf of bread and breaks off a chunk. It tears easily, though if he's been here for days it ought to be stale. To her surprise, he offers the chunk to her.

When she reaches for it, he jerks like he's been hit. "Your hands."

Most of the blood has worn off by now, but not all of it, and the cuts are easy to see. "I found some cliffs," she says, by way of explanation.

He reaches into his pack. "I have bandages. I can—"

"No." The refusal is instinctive. Letting him trap her hands like that . . . in theory he's her ally, at least a little, but theory dies with a knife in its back the moment she thinks about making herself vulnerable.

Aadet is staring at her. She says, "They'll be fine. Doesn't even hurt much any more. The bread?" She's less interested in the food than in distracting him.

She's also curious. The bread proves to be dry and not very flavorful, but nothing unusual happens when she swallows her first bite. So she says, "Luck?" and eats more. While she chews, she tugs off her boots and examines her feet. The leather is still damp, but it hasn't rubbed any blisters into her skin.

He's taken a second piece of bread for himself, and put the remainder back in his pack. "Luck . . . oh. Yes.

The island being here—I wasn't looking for it. I did a couple of years ago, but I'd given up. Seems like that's the way it is in the stories: people who look for the Lhian don't find her."

I sure as hell wasn't looking for her. Aadet offers a canteen; when she takes a sip, it proves to be water. *I wonder if the Cruais was.*

Testing his willingness to talk, she asks, "Where are you from, then?"

"Solaike," Aadet says. "And if I'm lucky again—if I can find the cave and make a deal with the Lhian—I'll have a reason to go back."

A note in his voice leaves her feeling hollow inside. It's the sound of a man hoping to see home again, after too long away. When she looks inside herself for that same hope, though, all she finds is emptiness. Not just an inability to remember home—which would be bad enough—but a certainty that there isn't one.

She hasn't really thought about where she'll go after this is done, because she doesn't truly believe the Cruais will let her go like he promised. Or that she'll even live to give him the chance. But the sense that she doesn't have anywhere to go *to* cuts deeply all the same.

Intending it to be cruel, she says, "You mean, if trailing along after me means I lead you to what you can't find on your own."

His fingers dig into the canteen. Their scraps of bread are long gone; she wonders how much more there is in that pack of his. The leather sack doesn't look very full or heavy. But he makes his voice light, saying, "I wouldn't complain. Who knows, though—maybe I'll be the one to lead *you* there."

She doubts it. But it isn't the hook that makes her get up and start walking again.

~

They're unquestionably on the slopes of the mountain now, which means the cave could be anywhere. She pauses, left hand resting comfortably on the hilt of her sabre, and looks up at the peak with a speculative eye. When Aadet reaches her side, she says, "What's happened to you so far? Since you got to the island."

"Are you asking what the Lhian has done to me?" She nods, and he blows his breath out in a long gust. "I thought I saw somebody early on, and kept trying to catch up with her, only I never could."

By the way he says it, she would lay a bet the woman he thought he saw was someone specific, and important to him. But he doesn't volunteer details, and she doesn't ask for any.

"Chasing that," Aadet says, "I nearly drowned in a bog,

that I'm pretty sure wasn't there until I was in the middle of it. And then later I found myself going back toward the shore—but that might have been an honest mistake."

She wonders if the obstacles are tailored to each visitor, or whether the Lhian merely follows her own whimsy. She can't really ask for Aadet's opinion, though, not without describing what's happened to her—and he hasn't said anything about winding up with keepsakes from his experiences. She can, however, say what she was thinking before. "Getting to the cave is clearly meant to be hard."

He follows her reasoning, and her line of vision. "You want to go straight up the mountain, rather than circling the lower slopes."

She shrugs. "Whatever choice we make first is likely to be wrong. If the Lhian can change things here, then she can put the cave wherever she damn well pleases, and make us fumble around until we've satisfied whatever arbitrary criteria she's set. But I'm betting it's higher up."

Out of the corner of her eye, she sees Aadet grinning. Scowling, she says, "What?"

"You said 'we,'" he says, and claps her on the shoulder as he goes by, committing himself to the upward path.

⌣

As much as it galls her to admit it, she'd have had a hell of a time getting up the mountain alone.

Not that she accepts Aadet's help when he offers it. Every time she thinks about taking his hand, she imagines what will happen if he lets go. Up here, she'd be lucky to get away with a broken leg; more likely she'd break everything, and not even badly enough that it would mean a quick death. But there are times when her grip fails or her boot slips, and Aadet's swift catch is the only thing that stops her from falling.

"You're used to doing this," she says through gritted teeth, inspecting her newly bruised elbow.

"We had to hide out in the mountains for a good two years before I was exiled," he answers. "And the only reason we lasted that long was, we were better at climbing than the soldiers were."

Better, but not perfect. He tires, as she does not. Eventually it happens that she scales a tall boulder, but his strength fails him. She looks down at him, and he up at her; she knows he's wondering the same thing she is. Whether she'll leave him there, and continue on her own.

If he hadn't caught her before, she might. But he did, and so she lays her sabre down, unties her sash. When she stretches out across the boulder's crown and lowers the cloth, he's able to climb high enough to grab it, and that little bit of assistance is enough to get him to the top.

He sprawls on the stone in much the same way she did when she cleared the cliffs. "Thank you," he says, breathing heavily. "And I'm sorry. I just—I need to rest."

There's apprehension in his voice. She can guess why. But if she was going to abandon him, she would have done it when he was at the base of the boulder. "Fine," she says, and goes looking for wood.

Her sabre isn't very well suited to chopping bushes, but she gathers enough to make a small fire, in an alcove she foolishly thought might be the cave entrance when she first saw it. Out of the wind, Aadet produces a striker from his pack and persuades the brush to burn, though it smokes foully from the damp. Once the fire is going, he huddles so close to it, she half-expects him to choke on the fumes.

She says, "I'm guessing Solaike is a warm land."

He shoots her an odd glance, but nods. "Very. I had a warmer shirt, but someone stole it—I'd washed it and left it out to dry, and then I dozed off." He shivers and hunches more tightly into himself. "I should have stolen another shirt, to go with that boat."

She studies him for a moment. He's the very picture of misery, exhausted and freezing, but she hasn't heard him say one word about giving up. "What are you hoping to accomplish, that's worth going through this?"

Aadet stares into the fire and doesn't answer.

After weighing the cost, she offers up another fragment of truth. "I wouldn't be here if I didn't have to be. I was sent here. Against my will."

As she predicted, it coaxes him into talking more. "My land needs a revolution. That's what I was trying to do—that's why I got exiled." He tucks his chin toward his chest. "I call it 'exile.' I should call it running away. Kaistun convinced me I had to go, had to get out of the country before they killed me. I used to think I should have stayed. Now . . . now I think that maybe this is why I left, though I didn't know it. Maybe the gods sent me out into the world so I could find the Lhian."

"You think she'll give you a revolution?"

"I think she'll give me the inspiration I need to start one, yes." Aadet is more animated now, the passion of his words warming him from within. "A generation ago, there was a military coup. This man named Valtaja, he'd been a general in the army, and he made himself king. We couldn't touch him—though we tried. The army was too loyal to him. But now he's dead, and it's his son who's holding the staff, and the soldiers aren't loyal to him the way they were to his father. He's vulnerable, I *know* it. The problem is, people these days are too used to knuckling under. I'm going to ask the Lhian for the words I need to *make* them stand up and fight back."

All this time, she's assumed he's there for the same thing she is: blood from the cauldron. Blood, words—how many things does the Lhian trade in?

Yet another thing the Cruais didn't see fit to tell her.

She probably won't live to take her anger out on him. Aadet, though, is right there. "So you've come here to get your people killed."

"What? No!"

Her lip curls in withering disdain. "I see. You know the secret to staging a revolution without anybody dying. Or is it that you think only the bad guys will die?"

Aadet glares at her, no longer curled in on himself. "I know there will be a price. But there's a price to staying as we are, too, and that one's worse."

"So *you* say. How about these people you want at your side, though? You want to *make* them stand up and fight back—that's what you said. Doesn't sound to me like you're going to leave them any choice."

It's a guess, but a calculated one. Nobody would row out to this island and drag themselves all over its treacherous landscape just for a lesson in rhetoric. What Aadet wants from the Lhian isn't just words; it's words that will have a specific effect, one that can't be resisted any more than she can resist the Cruais's command. And by his own admission, he'll use them to propel his people into a war that will get them killed.

He deflates by slow degrees, righteous anger decaying into horror.

"This king you're fighting only rules their bodies," she says, contemptuous. "You want to rule their minds."

Aadet whispers a phrase she can't understand. It sounds like an oath in his own language, or a prayer to the gods. "I—that isn't what I meant."

"Then you should consider your own words more carefully, before you go asking someone to give you new ones."

He buries his head in his hands, fingers gripping tight. "*Nikkor ja riest.* You're right. But—" He doesn't seem to know how to finish that sentence.

It's probably better that he stops talking. She's busy flinching back from her own mind, from all the echoes of *king* and *revolution* and *get your people killed.* She couldn't have said those things to him if she hadn't known them firsthand, once upon a time.

I don't think I want to remember any of that.

By the time Aadet looks up again, she's half-blind from staring into the fire, but it doesn't prevent her from seeing that his face is wet with tears. She wonders if he learned to cry silently while hiding from the soldiers. He says, "I can't give up, though. I've come this far. And I can't go home again—not unless I have a way to change things when I get there."

The word "home" twists inside her and almost provokes her into saying something vicious. But all that staring into the fire has done some good, because she's able to hear him with a calmer mind. The story he told has struck a chord inside her, catching her imagination, and she finds herself thinking it through. As if it were a puzzle she wants to solve. "Which do you care about more? Changing things, even if it means forcing it on those around you? Or letting your people choose—even if it means you might fail?"

He doesn't reply immediately. She respects him more for that. His horror at realizing what he would have done tells her what his answer will probably be, but he takes the time to consider it. Finally he says, "Letting them choose. Now that I know what I almost asked for . . . I couldn't live with myself, knowing I *forced* people into fighting. Into dying." He swallows and wipes his cheeks dry. "Do you mean I should give up? Go after this without the Lhian's help?"

"Hell no." She snorts. "Just ask for something different. Something that leaves them the choice."

There's an answer waiting to be spoken, like a bright light in her throat. She doesn't say it, though. Contempt was the right tone before, but now she wants to lead *him* to think of the possibility, not hand it to him on a platter. Besides . . . this might tell her what other kinds of deals the Lhian makes.

The Cruais bound her to get blood. But that doesn't necessarily mean she can't trade for something else, too—something for herself. It might tip the scales after she leaves the island.

But either Aadet is trapped in his original frame of thought, or the Lhian's stock in trade isn't limitless. "People don't believe a revolution is possible. I could ask her to give me *that* inspiration—the ability to make them see that it can be done. It doesn't force them to do anything, I think. It would just show them what I already see. I've tried to explain it before, but I've never really had the right words."

For the first time since she awoke in that stone circle, she feels like smiling. A real smile, not a threat with teeth. Aadet has seen it, the thing she wanted to suggest—and she helped him to it. She warns him, "They may not choose to fight. They may decide the cost is too high."

"Some probably will," Aadet admits. "But not all of them. It might be enough."

She doubts it will be. Despite her best efforts, she wasn't able to shed all those echoes in her mind: other revolutions, other leaders like Aadet. Many of them failed. Possibility is only the start; after that there needs to be planning, organization, a core strong enough to survive the inevitable shock of bloodshed and death. In the long run, Aadet might be better off asking the Lhian for a battle plan—assuming she can give him that kind of thing. But the best plan in the world won't do him much good if he can't get anyone to listen to him in the first place, so she thinks he's made the right choice.

He meets her eyes and says, "Thank you."

"For telling you that you're a fucking idiot?"

"Yes," he says, completely serious. "And for helping me see this differently. It isn't what I imagined would happen, when I suggested we travel together—but I'm glad you agreed. Instead of stabbing me and leaving me for dead." His smile is lopsided, rueful. "Even if you still don't trust me enough to tell me your name."

Her name might be buried somewhere in those blood-stained echoes. Who has she been, that she recalls so many revolutions? But she can't escape Therdiad's words: *Don't try to remember. The more you remember, the more you might end up losing.*

"Get some sleep," she says roughly, and lies down with her back to the tiny fire.

~

Whether she's incapable of sleep or just doesn't feel the need for it right now, she lies there for quite a while without anything happening.

On the other side of the fire, Aadet settles down. She can tell without looking that he'll be hunched into a ball, conserving what warmth he can. Did he have a blanket with him and lost it, or did he row across the bay without one? Either way, the cold probably won't kill him. He'll just be miserable and stiff when he gets up.

Helping him see his purpose differently . . . it felt *good*. It felt right, in the same way that the sash felt right, and the blade that lies within easy reach. Is this another gift of the island? A fellow traveler, someone whose path she can change? Or is it truly just chance that the two of them came here at the same time, found one another, decided to work together?

No way of knowing. She can't let go of the suspicion in her gut, though, the voice that tells her not to trust him. Aadet said that if the island wanted to trap him, it would have presented a damsel in distress, not a swordswoman. But if he's a trap for *her*, then the Lhian chose her tool well: a man dedicated to a cause, unflagging in the face of adversity, even though it's sure to get him killed sooner or later. He's someone she can work with, at least for a little while.

Everything good about this situation might be a sign of danger.

Not like there isn't danger everywhere she looks. Aadet, the island, the Lhian herself. *The more you remem-*

ber, the more you might end up losing. She's been able to ignore it most of the time, because she has so many other things to distract her: finding a path, fighting those creatures, hiding her ignorance from Aadet. But that hole is still inside her, a bottomless pit. She's already lost everything. What could possibly be so much worse that Therdiad would try to protect her from it?

Before she can stop herself, she reaches out, trying to capture—*something.* Anything. To take one of those echoes and make it solid, reclaim something that means more to her than vague recollections of deserts and war. But it's too late; she missed her chance, and all she grasps is void. The pain of that loss constricts her chest until she can't breathe. There's music in her mind, a wordless tune of lament; it sounds familiar, like a song she knew in the past, and the sorrowful weight of it is crushing her.

No. The music isn't in her mind.

She forces her eyes open. It's harder than dragging Aadet up that boulder, harder than dragging herself up the cliffs. There ought to be a great mass atop her, but there isn't: just the night air, lit faintly by the fire's last coals. She tries to inhale, and can't. Tries to move her limbs; the most she can manage is a weak, spasmodic twitch. She may not need food, and she may not need sleep . . . but she needs air, and the lack is turning her vision black at the edges.

She's made it this far, and now she's going to die because she let her guard down.

Her fingers scrabble in the dirt, hauling her leaden arms behind them, searching for something, *anything*. Her sabre, though it won't do her a damn bit of good when there's nothing to stab. She can't reach it.

Instead her left hand falls in the embers of the fire.

Pain sears through her scabbed palm. The music vanishes like a shadow in the light, and air comes rushing back into her lungs. She rolls onto her side, her knees, then lurches to her feet, swaying drunkenly. Breath has never tasted so sweet. She may expect to die here, but that doesn't mean she's resigned herself to it—not yet.

Aadet.

He's on his back when she turns to look at him, lying still. *Too still.* She can't hear the music, and there's nothing on top of him, but his chest doesn't look like it's moving.

She staggers over to him and drops to her knees once more. Up close, she can see the minuscule twitches, the signs that he's trying to draw breath and can't.

Pain's as good an answer as any. After all, it worked for her. The fingers of her left hand are still curled tight around the ember that burned her awake, and she thinks about trying to drag him to the fire. But that won't be easy, with her body still shaking from her own ordeal. Instead she draws back her right hand and delivers a full-armed slap to his face.

His head snaps to the side and his eyes fly open. She hears the gasp as he breathes in, his entire body jerking as if suddenly reinflated. Then Aadet begins to cough, curling in on himself.

She sinks back on her heels, her own heart beating too fast. Her left hand aches fiercely; she has to use the fingers of her other hand to pry it open. When she does, she finds the ember still glowing in her palm—but it is cool to the touch. Nor for that matter has it left a burn mark on her skin, though she feels the pain as if it has. She touches it gingerly with her right index finger. No pain now, but the light glows through the skin of her fingertip as if it were still burning.

She wants the warmth back, even if it hurt.

Aadet is on his hands and knees, shivering. She leaves him there, going to retrieve her sabre, which is cold as ice when she picks it up. The blade she slides through her sash once more; the ember she tucks inside the fabric as well, keeping her back to Aadet until it's out of sight. She doesn't want him asking what that thing is. It would be just one more question she can't answer. *It's mine. That's what matters.*

"What the hell was that?"

It takes her a moment to realize he's talking about the

suffocating music, not the ember. "Another test," she says, turning to face him. "One we nearly failed."

"You mean, one I *did* fail." He looks and sounds exhausted, worse than before, as if his sleep has done him no good at all. She wonders what he dreamt of, in those moments when he couldn't breathe. "I knew we should set guards, but I was too tired, and I didn't want to bother you." He sags back onto his heels. "Thank you. I owe you my life."

She thinks about saying they're even. After all, he helped her up the mountain, when falling would almost certainly have been lethal. But leverage over him may be useful. Instead she says, "We should move on."

He closes his eyes, lets his head droop. "You should go. If these are tests . . . who's to say the Lhian will even deal with me when I get there? Maybe I've already lost."

Aadet might still be useful—but that isn't why she crosses over to him. "Fuck that," she says, and drags him to his feet. "Give up now, and I'll kick you off this mountainside with my own boot. If the Lhian's going to refuse you, make her do it to your face."

~

They scale the peak, searching as they go for the cave that should be there.

Conversation has mostly died again, but their silence is born of exertion, rather than hostility and distrust. She helps Aadet when she has the better position, and he returns the favor. That tense knot in her gut never quite stops expecting him to let go at the worst possible moment . . . but she accepts the risk and gets on with what she has to do.

He never lets her go.

Countless shadows mark the mountainside, crevices and pits that might be the entrance to a cave. They have to check them all, because neither of them knows what the Lhian's cave is supposed to look like. Will it be natural, blending in with the surrounding landscape? Carved and framed with torches, a gateway to awe those who have found it at last? She starts to envision it as a maw, toothed with stalactites and stalagmites, ready to eat the fools who think they'll find what they seek within.

It doesn't look like any of these things. And Aadet finds it by accident.

He's standing in a precarious spot, craning his neck to see whether there's an opening farther up the slope, when his footing gives way. She lunges, but too late: all that time fearing he would let her fall, and it turns out she's the one who fails *him*. She listens, jaw clenched, to the sliding rocks and snapping brush and yelped curses that mark his descent, and curls her hands into fists when silence follows. Then Aadet's voice comes up from below, dry with self-mockery: "I think I've found it."

There might be an easier path than the one he took, but she doesn't feel like searching for it. Knowing this place, she would never find him, or the cave, again. So she crouches and follows in Aadet's wake, slightly more controlled, but arriving at the foot of the slope bruised all the same. *A few more marks for my growing collection.*

The cave mouth is neither natural, nor particularly remarkable. It has the uneven edge of the other places they've searched, with a litter of dirt and leaves stretching inward, carried by the wind. There are no torches. But the floor is flat and the tunnel, which should be dark just a few feet in, has the same sourceless glow that lit the forest earlier. And there is a stillness to the air that isn't simply a lack of breeze: it's expectation, anticipation. This is the heart of the Lhian's domain. *Something* will happen inside. It only remains to find out how bad that something will be.

Aadet takes off his pack, pulls out his canteen, offers it to her. She shakes her head, not looking away from the cave mouth. He shrugs and drains the last of it. If the journey off the island is a quarter as difficult as the journey here, he'll regret having to hunt for more water. But she understands why he does it. Going in to face the Lhian . . . he wants to be prepared.

She doesn't even know *how* to prepare. There's just a ghost in her memory, one that says she's never been here before . . . but all the same, she feels like she's seen it, or something much like it, in the past.

Don't try to remember.

It's safer if you don't remember.

She snarls and moves forward, not looking to see if Aadet follows.

Before long she can hear his footsteps behind hers, echoing off the stone walls. The tunnel curves, eclipsing the faint moonlight that fills the entrance. Every muscle in her body is loose and ready, hand drifting near the hilt of her sabre. This would be the ideal place for an ambush: one final trial, before the traveler is allowed to reach the Lhian.

But nothing attacks. There is only the sound of their footsteps, and that ever-present glow . . . and then, up ahead, a brighter light.

She rounds the final curve, and knows they have reached their mark.

The chamber does not look anything like natural. Its walls and ceiling are rough, the latter toothed with stalactites—but the stalactites hang in regular, concentric circles, and the floor below is smooth as glass. The glow is stronger here, and strongest around a black, rounded shape at the center of the cave.

The cauldron. This is what the Cruais sent her to find.

She half-expects the hook buried in her spirit to drag her forward the instant she sees the cauldron, but no: she stands frozen, staring, with Aadet just behind her right shoulder.

Laughter echoes through the chamber.

A woman steps into view. Inhumanly tall, her skin white as bone, her hair red as blood. Her nails are pointed like claws. She is the one laughing, and the sight of her feels like the ground dropping away. Unquestionably she is the Lhian . . . and she is *familiar.*

Not familiar in the way of a person previously met. No, the Lhian is nowhere in those ghostly echoes of memory. But there is a resonance there—a kinship. A sense that the two of them share some connection, and Aadet does not.

It's her the Lhian is laughing at. The tall woman comes to the edge of the stalactites and brings her hands together in slow, mocking applause. "I see the Cruais has become more creative in his tactics," she says. Her voice is melodious and cold, reminiscent of the music that nearly killed them not long ago. "He has tired of sending people, and losing them; and so he sends *you.*"

Aadet is staring at them both, gaze snapping back and forth, his lips parting as understanding dawns. He whispers that phrase again, the one that must be an oath to his gods. "I should have guessed," he says, staring at the person he has traveled so far with. "You're like her. Not human. You're an archon."

The word hits like a hammer, slamming open the doors she's been trying so hard to keep closed. She can't blame him for speaking it, though. The word was there anyway, hovering at the edge of her thoughts, ever since she saw the Lhian. *Archon.*

Other memories come flooding in. Of course Aadet is right; of course she isn't human, though she has the shape of one. She is an entity born out of story and dream, summoned from the realm of the apeiron by a ritual the Cruais performed, given flesh so that she may be bound to this task, the challenge that killed so many of his own people. When she dies, it is to the apeiron she will return, until another mortal calls her forth.

"Did I even exist before that moment?"

"No."

"Yes."

The desert, the sea, the knowledge of pistols and the familiar sensation of her stride settling into a comfortable rhythm. Languages and echoes of revolution. All from previous lives, earlier rounds of existence, before she died and lost it all again.

None of that tells her why remembering is dangerous . . . but the answer must have to do with the Lhian.

This island—it isn't a normal place, part of the ordinary world in which humans live. It's the Lhian's domain. Which means the Lhian is free, not bound to any human's will. Was she freed by her summoner, the way the Cruais pretended he would free his own summoned slave? Or did she break the binding on her own?

It doesn't really matter. All that matters is, the Lhian is free, and vastly more powerful. Everything in her domain operates by her rules, according to her own archetypal nature . . . and the few shreds of information Aadet shared on the way here are not enough to make that nature clear.

Knowledge is strength. Memory is strength. The more she recalls, the stronger she will be—but no, they told her not to, they swore she would be safer in ignorance. Were they lying? Her gut screams that they were. But a tiny point of fire burns into her side, the ember from the fire, and she grips it as she wrenches herself back from the brink. Mentally, and physically: she stumbles a few steps, even though she was standing still on a smooth floor.

"By my name," the Lhian says, a delighted smile curving her perfect lips. "You didn't know, did you?" Her laughter rings out again, bright and insincere. "How clever of the Cruais! To send an archon, so newly summoned that she is ignorant even of her own nature. And yet you made it across the island, blind, deaf, and dumb

as you are. Owing to the good efforts of this one, perhaps?"

Aadet tenses when the Lhian's gaze falls upon him.
His hands rise slightly, as if to seek the comfort of his
knives.

"No," the Lhian says thoughtfully. "I do not think he
can rightfully claim all of the credit. The Cruais did well,
then, when he summoned you. They often don't, you
know. The art of summoning an archon is *so* imprecise."
Her smile is predatory. She is a cat with a mouse between
her paws, secure enough in her power to enjoy herself.
"But of course you don't know. How thoughtless of me to
say such things."

She wants to snatch out her blade and take the Lhian's
head off in the same movement, then grab blood from
the cauldron and run. It would be pure suicide, of course:
she doesn't stand a chance in hell of defeating a more
powerful archon in the heart of that archon's own domain. But she isn't sure whether it's self-preservation instinct or the Cruais's binding that stops her from trying
anyway.

The sabre. The sash. The ember. There's no point hiding those things from Aadet any longer; they've made
it to the cave, and if he's going to stop trusting her, it
won't be because she picked up a few unnatural trin-
kets along the way. "Do I have you to thank for these?"

she asks, pulling the ember from her sash, gesturing at her other acquisitions.

The Lhian's mouth hardens. "No—and you should be glad of it. Those, I fear, are merely the consequence of my island responding to the presence of another archon, which it has not felt in many long years."

That reply answers more than one question. The Lhian, she thinks, would have taken credit for those gifts if she could. Credit, and payment. The fact that she didn't suggests that she *can't*—that even here, in her place of power, she is bound by her own nature. *As every archon is,* she thinks, remembering what Aadet said, matching it with the knowledge she's regained. Trying not to step any further into her own mind than she has to. *We can't be what we aren't.* The Lhian extracts a price for everything she gives, but it is not in her nature to cheat.

Which isn't the same thing as playing fair.

But it makes her feel better about the weight on her hip. They mean something to her, these things she won during her journey: they're symbols of her own nature, just like the cauldron is a symbol of the Lhian's. Even if she doesn't understand their significance, their presence comforts her. She isn't quite as empty inside as she used to be.

No doubt that will end up biting her on the ass before long.

Aadet has been silent throughout this, ever since he named his companion for what she is. He drifted a step or two away while the two archai spoke, watching them with a wary eye; now he steps forward, shoulders back and tense with determination. Facing the Lhian, he demands, "Have I fulfilled your conditions? Or are you going to say I cheated, because an archon helped me?"

Don't give her that opening, you fool. But the Lhian merely smiles again. She looks genuinely amused—but not at Aadet. It doesn't bode well. "Those who come to my island may use any tool at their disposal to win through. You stand before me; you may make your request."

Aadet glances back over his shoulder. It's almost touching, that he looks to her for confirmation, even though he knows she's been lying to him this entire time. Never mind that she didn't know she was an archon: she knew plenty of other things she didn't say, any one of which would probably have let him figure it out far sooner. But she also told him what he needed to hear, and apparently he's still grateful for that.

It is the Lhian he must speak to, not her. He faces forward again and says, "I've heard tales where you misinterpret the things people say, because they didn't speak carefully enough. So I'm going to be *very* clear."

The Lhian's face is impassive, but her eyes gleam, as if Aadet has spotted a trap. *No, she doesn't play fair.*

With a few simple strokes, he draws the outline of the situation he described before, when the two of them sat on opposite sides of that tiny fire. The history of his country, and the tyranny of the man who rules over them now. "I want to show my people that a revolution is possible," Aadet says. "I'm not going to lie to them; I don't want to make them see hope where it doesn't exist. And I don't want to force them to do anything they don't choose freely. But I want to open their eyes, so they see the possibility that's in front of them. They've let fear and despair blind them for too long."

He kneels, hands clasped over his raised knee, and says, "I beg you for the inspiration necessary to do this."

There are loopholes, if the Lhian wants to exploit them. If Aadet is wrong—if the revolution he dreams of is no more than wishful thinking, doomed to failure in the real world, and the only hope that exists is imaginary—then he might get nothing from this. He might show them what is possible, but the cost will be so high that even thinking of it will destroy all hope of change for a generation to come. And beyond that, a great deal will depend on what price the Lhian asks in return.

But it's still a damned sight better than what he originally came here to do. Even if the Cruais's mission ends in failure, she accomplished that much.

The Lhian inclines her head in a gracious nod, a queen

showing charity to a beggar. "Very well. Pay, and what you ask for will be yours."

No negotiation. Her gut tenses as Aadet stands. He seems to know what to do; he strides without hesitation to the cauldron, which stands at the precise center of the cave. The light illuminates him from below as he looks into its depths.

Then he holds out his left arm, draws a knife with his other hand, and slices his skin open.

Blood pours into the cauldron below: not enough to kill him, but enough to hurt. And she, watching, understands at last the trap the Cruais sent her into.

Aadet has asked the Lhian for the inspiration necessary to rally his people. The price for that, it seems, is the price she extracts from all who ask beg for inspiration: blood.

The Cruais sent his chained archon to obtain blood.

The price will be inspiration.

Horror renders her mute and inert. She is an archon. Her very soul is a story, told over and over again through one lifetime after another, each rendition a variation on the same, fundamental theme: a particular kind of inspiration, given flesh. To pay the Lhian's price is to surrender a piece of *herself*.

"*The more you remember . . . the more you might end up losing.*"

No doubt Therdiad was sincerely trying to help. But will ignorance really protect her? Maybe it doesn't matter that she's newly summoned, so lost to her own nature after the non-being of the apeiron that she didn't even know she was an archon until Aadet told her. Does she have to know her own story before the Lhian can take it? Or can the Lhian carve out her payment regardless, claiming something she doesn't even know is there, leaving a hole she'll never be able to fill if she lives for a thousand years?

She doesn't know. And it doesn't matter. She is bound, condemned to make this deal even at the cost of her own soul.

If by some unlikely chance she succeeds, and returns to the Cruais with the blood he demanded ... then she will destroy everything she can before he binds her to stop or unmakes her entirely. She never believed his promise to let her go free. It happens sometimes, that people free the archai they summoned—but not this time. Even if he means to follow through, he'll change his mind when she claims her revenge, in blood a thousand times over.

Aadet goes to the Lhian, kneels once more. *Don't do it!* she wants to scream at him—but he has already paid his price. Now comes his reward. The Lhian sets her fingertips gently against his temples and closes her eyes. There is no more outward sign than that: no light flashes, no sound breaks the stillness of the air. Aadet doesn't even shiver. The two of them might be a statue carved from a single stone. Then he inhales suddenly, as if the music had paralyzed him again, and a spike of pain has now broken its spell. The Lhian lowers her hands, and Aadet, wide-eyed, climbs to his feet.

He grips his arm as he comes to stand at her side once more, pressing to stop the flow of blood. He was intelligent in how he made the cut, at least; it won't bleed for much longer, and won't leave his arm any worse for the wear.

She herself will not be so lucky.

"You never told me what you came here for," he says, voice low. "Only that someone else sent you. But I wouldn't have made it here without your aid, and I owe you for that. If I can help you in some way—without risking my own people—I will."

Wouldn't that be a pretty irony: she takes from the cauldron the same blood he just gave, and in exchange the Lhian reclaims the inspiration she granted only seconds ago. But no, he won't do that, and she wouldn't ask it anyway. Not when he is exactly what he claimed to be: an ordinary human, facing an archon's trials in order to help his people. Not when he kept faith with her, against all her expectations and what she deserves.

What if she sold something else out of his mind, leaving him what he came here for?

She looks past him, to the Lhian. "There's no point in dancing around it. You know I'm here for blood."

"Of course," the Lhian says. She does not smile. "Do you know why?"

Because I don't have a choice. But that isn't what the Lhian is asking. She clamps her mouth shut, not willing to play her part. She doesn't trust the Lhian not to extract blood in payment for the answer.

Aadet tells her what she needs to know. "Prophecy," he says, his voice quiet and rough. "One drop of blood gives the gift of speaking a single prophecy. Or so the stories say."

The vial hanging from the cord around her neck won't hold much blood, but it will hold more than a single drop. She wonders why the Cruais didn't send her with a jug. Under the circumstances, restraint seems pointless.

If the Lhian is annoyed by Aadet's interference, she doesn't let it show. She merely says, "You know what the price will be."

Aadet is still at her side. She says, "If you want to help—"

She never finds out what he would have said. The Lhian's voice cracks the air of the cave, cold and enormous, driving them both to their knees. *"Do not play games.* You will pay the price—you and no other."

The reverberations of it echo down her bones, leaving her shaking. For an instant she feels the vast gulf between them, the archon who rules this place and the one who has barely survived to reach it. Cat and mouse doesn't begin to describe it: she is a new leaf on a tree, and the Lhian is the hurricane that can strip the tree bare.

But she refuses to cower. She climbs to her feet, unsteady; then she bends and helps Aadet up. "I had to try," she whispers in his ear. He doesn't answer.

So. Nothing has changed: she still has no choice, no path forward except the one laid down for her. Get the blood, pay the price—or fail. The man who survived, the one who came back empty-handed . . . was the inspiration of a human not enough to pay the Lhian's price? Or did he lose something precious in the journey? Did he make it this far, get the blood—and then forfeit the memory of the reason he came here in the first place?

She doesn't have to remember. The binding will force her to follow through on her task, no matter what shell remains when the Lhian is done taking her cut. She is a puppet, and nothing more.

Which means she loses nothing by pushing. The Lhian might kill her—but is that really worse than the alternative? "Aadet cut his own arm. He chose how much to bleed for you. Do I get to choose how much I pay?"

She half-expects the Lhian's voice to ring out again, worse than before. But the other archon merely says, "No. It is not often that I give blood from my cauldron to those who ask. That is not my purpose, nor my desire. You have done what you must, and so I will trade with you—but on *my* terms." Her mouth lifts slightly in contempt. "You do not even understand yourself well enough to make an acceptable offer."

It's unfortunately true. Maybe if she hadn't held back before—if she'd chased the memories, clawed back every scrap of her self that she could—but even then, no. As the Lhian says, they are trading on *her* terms. Remembering would only have made her aware of what she's about to lose.

She wants to bargain. Wants to refuse. Wants to spit in the Lhian's face and walk out of here.

She can't.

"All right," she says, though her jaw is clenched so tight it hurts.

The Lhian extends one gracious hand, gesturing toward the cauldron. "Then there is what you seek. You may take what you came for."

There is a warning in the Lhian's voice—but what the warning is, she doesn't know. She walks under the stalactites toward the cauldron, pausing just underneath the inner ring. The space before her glows with cool, silver light. The cauldron is tall enough that she cannot see inside, but she knows without looking that it's full of blood: far more blood than a vessel that size should hold, because it contains every deal the Lhian has ever made, every price paid by those desperate to buy inspiration at any cost.

Minus whatever few drops the Lhian has traded away before. She wonders what inspiration those people sacrificed, in exchange for the blood they took.

All of that is her stalling. The hook buried in her soul pulls at her, dragging her forward. The cauldron is seven steps away. Seven steps, and she will have what she needs.

She draws in a deep breath, and takes the first step.

~

Something flickers at the edge of her vision.

It is ephemeral: a mere wisp, like warm breath in cold air. But it tantalizes her, distracting her from the cauldron ahead. She wants to reach out and take hold of it.

So that's the trick.

The Lhian told her to take what she came for—which is blood, and blood alone. If she takes anything else . . .

Then she will have broken the deal. What the penalty for that would be, she doesn't know, but it won't stop at mere inspiration. In all likelihood, she will forfeit herself entirely to the Lhian.

She grits her teeth and takes a second step.

The flicker is still there. Stronger. And there's another on the opposite side of her vision, more tempting than the first. They feel familiar, those wisps of thought—familiar like the sabre, the red sash around her waist, the ember from the fire. Like they belong to her, if only she would claim them.

You know better than that. Nothing she can offer you is worth that mistake.

A third step—and now she *knows* what it is that taunts her, luring her to give in and break the bargain she made. The Lhian deals in two things: blood, and inspiration. This is the latter, of course ... but the Lhian is diabolically clever. Mere random ideas would hold little temptation. No, this is far worse.

What the flickering cloud of thoughts offers is no less than everything she has lost.

Her memories. Her *self*. The countless lives she's lived—all the times humans have summoned her from the apeiron, then banished her back to it. Or freed her. Or she won her way free on her own. There will be instances of each in those flickers, she is sure, because archai are eternal; in the countless years of her countless lives, she will have experienced all those things and more. But in every lifetime, the core of her self will have been the same. And that knowledge can be hers—if she just gives in.

She fixes her gaze on the cauldron and steps forward again.

The hook doesn't help. The binding on her drives her to complete the task whether she wants to or not, but it can't protect her from failing. If her own mistakes had killed her out on the island, that would have been the end of this life, and the Cruais would never get what he summoned her for. She can't *decide* to say "to hell with the blood" and accept the Lhian's temptation . . . but if her own weakness or stupidity breaks her, then she will be lost, and never mind what the Cruais wants.

She must do this on her own strength, or not at all.

She takes the fifth step.

It only gets stronger. They're crowding around her now, all the memories she dares not even look at. She walks through a storm of her own self, vision narrowing to a pinpoint, afraid to even blink for fear that when she opens her eyes, she will see something she should not, and the Lhian will interpret that as theft. Her arms are rigid at her sides, hands packed tight into fists, so that no trailing finger can touch a stray wisp. Only two steps more.

Another—and now she hears a voice, whispering seductively in her ear. *It can take an archon years, even a century or more, to reach their full strength, because they do not know who they are. They do not remember enough. But with a true understanding of yourself . . . how powerful would you be? You have a blade at your side. Could you not challenge the Lhian, and win?*

She cannot tell whether that voice is the Lhian's, or her own.

Every muscle in her body cramps with tension. All she has to do is reach out, and all of this can be hers. She can be whole again—perhaps more whole than she has been for lifetimes, her existence too often cut short by death. She tries to tell herself that the Lhian is lying, that these memories are false, there's no way that treacherous bitch can know her more profoundly than she knows herself. But she can't be sure it's true. What lies within the other archon's power, and what does not? Maybe the visions all around her are real.

They aren't what she came here for. Aching inside with the emptiness she cannot—must not—*will* not fill, she takes the final step.

It's like breaking through the surface of water to open air. She gasps in what feels like her first breath in a century, body shaking from head to toe. There is nothing around her now, only the cold, brilliant light of the cauldron, which stands on a low pedestal before her.

The binding, or perhaps the Cruais, has this much mercy: she's allowed to gather her strength, instead of immediately being compelled forward. She wonders if he knew what temptation the Lhian would put in her path, and how hard it would be to refuse.

Not the latter. No human can truly understand it, because their souls are not the same. They choose who to be: an archon cannot.

When she is sure her knees will hold her, she mounts the pedestal and looks down into the cauldron.

Lightning spiderwebs through her body once more, following the path of her blood. She felt it before, when she saw the dead bull the Cruais used to summon her, when she touched the stain of her own blood on the moss and it rose up in her fingers as red cloth.

This is why he got *her*, when he sounded his horn through the apeiron and summoned an archon to help him. It's hard for such a ritual to be precise, unless the summoner is very skilled; he might have gotten any one of a hundred archai, all variants on the theme of his need. But he used blood to call her, and blood is at the core of her nature, in ways she doesn't understand. For one fleeting moment, she finds herself strangely glad that she *isn't* here to ask for inspiration. As much as she dreads what the Lhian will do with a piece of her soul, her blood might not be any better. Might even be worse.

She can't stay here. She has to collect what she came for, and then return it to the Cruais. Only then will her task be done—and her path will end in the freedom he promised, or the death she expects.

Reaching into the neck of her shirt, she pulls out the bone vial he gave her. It's the work of a moment to unloop its cord and tug the stopper free. When she dips it into the cauldron, the blood rises before she even nears its surface: a thin red stream that flows obediently against gravity, in through the tiny neck of the vial, until it is full. She holds her breath, watching it move, and exhales only when the flow stops. Then she closes the vial, puts it back around her neck, and turns to go back the way she came.

She can't see anything past the glow; everything beyond is shadow. But assuming the cave hasn't changed, it's seven steps back to the inner ring of stalactites.

She takes the first step—and realizes the Lhian is not yet done.

The visions are back, even stronger than before. They call up every ache within her: the hollowness of ignorance and absence of choice, the helplessness of being bound by someone who doesn't care who or what she is, so long as she can be a useful tool. She burns to be *herself* again, not this sad, pathetic little echo, scarcely more than human.

And she can be. All she has to do is accept what the Lhian offers.

It isn't the binding that stops her. It isn't a fear that the visions are nothing more than empty promises and lies. It isn't even the awareness that if she gives in, she will have lost, no matter how much she gains in return. Maybe she could defeat the Lhian, maybe she couldn't—but she doesn't really care.

What stops her is a pure, searing refusal to accept her own soul from someone else's hands.

Fuck her, and fuck her "gifts." I don't need her help, or anybody else's. If she offered this to me for free, I'd throw it back in her face. I will know myself again; I will remember everything I have lost, and return to my true self. But I will do it on my own.

She holds that thought around her like armor, putting it between herself and the world, repeating it like a mantra with every step she takes. It doesn't break the storm that fills the air; the visions are still there, still every bit as entrancing as before. Worse. She would weep, but her fury burns the tears away before they can fall. Seven steps to the cauldron, and seven steps back; and the return journey makes those first seven feel like *nothing*. But there's a fire raging inside her now, an inferno that drowns out any other voice except the one that says she *will* do this, and to hell with the Lhian, to hell with everything—all that matters is that she *will . . . get . . . through.*

~

And then the glow fades, and she is standing beneath the stalactites once more, with a single syllable echoing through her mind:

Ree.

She goes blind from the resonance, swaying on her feet. That brief sound is like a bell, echoing into the deepest reaches of her spirit. It is a piece of her true name—a fragment only. The rest is still out of her reach. But for the first time since the Cruais called her into being atop that ritual stone, Ree knows who she is.

A wanderer—that's what he wanted from the apeiron. Someone whose nature was to make an impossible journey, and return. A warrior, too, capable of defending himself or herself, because that would be necessary; but it was the journey he was thinking of, more than the danger, and so he got her. Because she will never make a domain for herself, as the Lhian has done here. There is no home for her, now or ever. She will always move on, and overcome whatever is in her path . . . or die trying.

He called for someone like her, and he called with blood. And so he got Ree.

Fear spikes through her like ice. *I shouldn't know these things. I can't take anything she offered—*

But this isn't from the Lhian. She knows these things about herself because she found them within, because they came with that fragment of her name. What she just did—those seven steps to the cauldron and seven steps back, driving herself beyond her limits because she refused to fail—was a moment of perfect harmony, an echo of her truest self. Among all those distant memories of failure and death, there are moments where she succeeded.

A familiar sight, like a sabre or a gun, can make her remember trivial things; this can do more. And she won her name from the apeiron, not from the Lhian.

That realization brings with it another one: she is no longer bound.

Ree is too breathless to laugh at the terrible irony of it. The Cruais trapped her spirit with his summoning ritual . . . but by reclaiming a piece of her own name, she's broken free of that net. She has the blood in a vial around her neck, and she can do anything she wants with it: drink it. Pour it out. Give it to Aadet. Turn and hurl the vial back into the cauldron and tell the Lhian she changed her mind—she doesn't want the blood after all, and their deal is null and void.

She doesn't have to pay.

When she looks up, she finds Aadet staring at her. What the hell her struggle looked like from the outside, she doesn't know—did he see the visions swarming around her? Or just Ree, body tensed as if against a gale-force headwind in a perfectly still cave? Maybe she vanished from his sight entirely. But judging by the way he's staring, probably not.

Ree's looking at him because she doesn't want to look at the Lhian.

She has to decide, right now. Not what to do with the blood if she keeps it—she can think about that later. But she has to make up her mind whether she will keep it or not. Whether she will pay the price. A single fragment of her true name doesn't make her anywhere near strong enough to fight the Lhian and win.

A little while ago she might have done it anyway, just out of a sheer, self-annihilating impulse to escape this trap. The binding stopped her then. Now ... now she thinks that maybe she isn't ready to die after all.

Is she ready to lose a piece of herself?

The mere prospect nauseates her. Ree knows herself now, at least a little. She isn't just an archon, and therefore a story that repeats throughout the ages; she is a *teller* of stories, someone whose voice has its own power. She felt the faintest echo of it when she talked with Aadet over the fire, turning him away from his foolish request and toward a better one. When she comes fully into her strength, maybe he won't need someone like the Lhian. Ree won't hand him what he's looking for, but she'll lead him toward it, awakening the fire in his spirit so he can awaken others in turn. What part of her nature will she lose, if she keeps the vial of blood?

The more she thinks about it, the more reasons she has to throw the vial back. Every reason, in fact, except for one.

If she does that, then she will have made that journey, seven steps there and seven steps back, for nothing.

Yes, she got her name out of it, and the first, tentative understanding of herself. But she didn't do it for those things. She did it for the blood. For the Cruais and his people—who may or may not be worth what she's gone through. But it was their summoning that brought her here, that gave her life once more. And if she throws the blood back, she'll never find out why.

Therdiad at least had thanked her. And he did what he could to protect her against the Lhian.

Too bad it didn't work.

Ree curls one hand around the vial and turns to face the Lhian.

The other archon's expression is unreadable. She says, "Do you have what you seek?"

When Ree answers, she is preternaturally aware of her own voice. How will it sound, after this moment? Her gut twists, but she says the words anyway. "I do. So get on with it."

The Lhian gestures. Ree approaches, kneels, braces herself for agony.

Cool fingertips touch her brow—and the world changes.

~

They are still in the cave, with that cold, silver light . . . but it is as if the sun has emerged from behind a cloud.

Color comes flooding in, and life, and warmth. Things she didn't know were missing until they came back. Ever since the Cruais summoned her, she's known with a cold, unrelenting fatalism that no matter what happens, she's fucked. Now it lifts, as if burned away by the fire she called on when she refused the Lhian's temptation. One hand goes instinctively to the ember tucked into the sash at her waist. If the sabre is the icy certainty of death, the ember is the fire that burns on regardless. It is a piece of herself, one that had dwindled down to almost nothing. Now that fire comes roaring back, bringing with it the possibility that she might just survive this—even come out of it stronger.

Ree staggers to her feet, backing away from the Lhian.

"What the hell did you just take from me?"

She should sound horrified, but she doesn't. Horror is impossible, in the face of the lightness that now suffuses her. And in a way, that's *more* frightening: it's like she's drunk, and too far gone to realize the danger she's in.

The Lhian's smile suggests she knows all of this. "Nothing, I think, that you will miss."

"The hell I won't," Ree says wildly, not even sure how angry she should be. "Do you expect me to believe you just did—*whatever* you did—for my own benefit? Because you're so kind and generous?"

"Not at all," the Lhian replies, unperturbed. "But there is such a thing as a mutually beneficial deal. Is it so impossible to believe that is what I have given you?"

Impossible, no . . . but unlikely, yes. Ree hasn't lost *all* suspicion and self-preservation instinct. But when she looks inside herself, comparing what she feels now against the impressions she had before, she can't tell what might be missing. Rather—

When Aadet spoke of "aspects" before, on their way up the mountain, it meant nothing—because she didn't realize the word applied to her. But she feels it within herself, the duality of an archon's nature: the force of creation, and the force of destruction. Which aspect currently rules the Lhian, she can't begin to guess . . . but Ree herself has been in the latter, ever since the Cruais summoned her.

Until now. Somehow, whatever the Lhian took, it has changed her over to the other side. From ice to fire, from the conviction of death to the hope of survival.

"I did not take *that* from you," the Lhian says, before Ree can ask. It has to be true. If she'd taken half of Ree's soul, the destructive aspect that awaits a knife in the back, then Ree wouldn't be frantically analyzing this deal now, searching for the hidden flaw. But that side has retreated, and she isn't nearly as afraid as she should be.

She still wants to know what she's lost. But it's hard to fight the joy bubbling up within her, the feeling that an enormous burden has been taken from her shoulders, leaving her as light as a feather. Will she truly miss whatever is gone?

I'm sure that someday I will.

But for now . . .

Ree touches the vial of blood around her neck. Although she doesn't need the Cruais to free her anymore, she's curious to see what he will do when she brings this back. Once she and Aadet find a way off the island, of course.

"We aren't done," she warns the Lhian. "I'll be back someday."

The Lhian's smile reminds her of a hunting cat. "Come prepared to pay for what you take."

Blood, to get back whatever she's lost. It isn't a good deal; she'll have to find some other way. But at least now she believes another way might exist. "Are we free to go?"

One bone-white hand gestures toward the exit, and the Lhian sinks into a mocking bow. Ree doesn't bother returning it as she walks, with Aadet, out into the night.

~

It wouldn't have surprised Ree if the Lhian made them fight for every hundred paces they take toward the shore, but she doesn't. The trip is still less than easy—they're both bruised anew before they get down off the mountain—but it goes ten times more quickly than it did on the way in, and no strange creatures trouble them as they pass.

Aadet even manages to find the boat he rowed over from the mainland. It's a round, flat-bottomed thing, barely large enough to hold the two of them. When Aadet casts a speculative eye toward Ree, she snorts. "Sorry. If I've paddled a boat in some other lifetime, I don't remember it yet." But she takes the job of pushing them out into the water, getting wet up to the hips before she jumps in and Aadet sets to work with his oar.

The water is still preternaturally calm and dark; the sun has only risen in Ree's soul. The island vanishes quickly into the mist as Aadet paddles them away. When it's gone, he makes a sound of rueful frustration and says, "I should have known you were an archon."

"*I* should have known," she says dryly. "But the people who summoned me did their damnedest to keep me as ignorant as they could. They thought it would help." And maybe it did. She scrapes dried blood off her palms, careful of the scabs. Then she adds, "My name is Ree. I know that now. And I'm sorry for not telling you anything before."

He waves that away, in between strokes of the oar. "You saved my life—and my purpose. That more than makes up for it. Can I at least let you off wherever you need to go?" He pauses and cranes his neck around the waters of the bay, which have started to rise into ordinary waves. "Assuming you know where that is, because I sure as hell don't."

Neither does Ree. But as the sky begins to brighten—dawn, at last—they hear a voice ringing out over the waters: "Hey! Over here!"

It's Therdiad in his rowboat, looking tired but cautiously happy. He rows toward them, and Aadet paddles to meet him, until the two vessels come alongside and Ree grabs their edges to keep them from drifting. Incredulous, she says, "Have you been sitting out here this entire time? However long it's been."

"Five nights," Therdiad says. "And no, not the whole time. The island only appears at night. During the day, I go back to shore."

So he wasn't just planning to abandon her on the island, leaving her to find her own way back. Ree wishes she had thought to ask earlier—but she probably wouldn't have believed him anyway. "Mind taking on some passengers?" she asks, and Therdiad waves them both in.

He rows the rest of the way back to shore, with the round little boat bobbing on a line behind. She can see other craft on the water as the sun begins to rise; Therdiad casts a worried glance in their direction and rows harder. "I feel like I should return my boat," Aadet says, biting his lip.

"You did pay for it," Ree points out. "Like you just said: it's your boat, now."

"Not that I have any use for it after this," he answers with a laugh. "I don't fancy trying to cross the ocean in it. Maybe I should sell it to somebody else? I could use the money; it's a long way home."

When Therdiad runs his craft aground on the shore, Ree splashes in again to pull it up higher. They can't do much to conceal it, but he's also taken her to a different stretch of the coast than before, she thinks. Farther from the village. "We had to hide," Therdiad explains. "The local Cruais *really* doesn't like people trying to go to the Lhian's island."

He hasn't asked whether Ree has the blood. She probably couldn't have left the island if she didn't . . . but she likes that he hasn't asked. He trusts her. Even now, that feels a little strange.

But it's a strangeness she could learn to enjoy.

They find Ectain cul Simnann and his people camped out in a shallow bowl of land, where they can at least light a fire without it being visible for miles. Every one of them leaps to their feet when the three travelers approach, though Ree can see them staring dubiously at Aadet. *Probably wondering what part of my anatomy I pulled* him *out of.* Either that, or the Lhian does a side trade in healthy young men.

The Cruais approaches, leaning on a stick, with everyone else trailing behind. Ree's been thinking about this the whole way back, and acts before he can speak. She takes the vial from around her neck and tosses it to him.

He drops the stick and nearly falls over his own feet, rushing to catch the precious object. Ree suppresses the urge to grin: he may or may not be able to recognize the difference between her two aspects, but she doesn't want to clue him in that something has changed. No, the idea here is to see what he does next.

Ectain cul Simnann, Cruais of his people, doesn't

waste any time. He opens the vial, sees the blood inside, and nods. Looking directly at her, he says, "Archon of unknown name, I free you from your service to me and mine."

She doesn't feel anything. Of course not: the cord he's trying to cut snapped back in the Lhian's cave. But it tells her what she needs to know.

"You're a man of your word," she says. "Unnecessary, as it turns out—I freed myself, with no help from you." *Or from the Lhian.* "But I'm glad to know you meant it."

He blanches. Probably he's remembering the threat she made before leaving, and imagining what she might have done to him and his if he tried to go back on his word. Or even what she's going to do now. But Ree's anger toward him has faded from what it was before.

Faded—but not entirely gone. "Did you know what she would take from me?"

The Cruais looks down. "In specific, no. In general . . . yes." His shoulders slump. "Forgive me. Our people tried, repeatedly, and failed. I thought only an archon could win through. It seemed worth the chance—even though I knew the cost to you would be terrible."

Aadet got through, she thinks. But then again, Aadet wasn't there for blood.

The Cruais struggles briefly with himself, then loses the fight. "What you were made to give up, in exchange for this. Is there . . . can we make you whole somehow?"

His tone isn't optimistic. Ree doubts he could do anything, even if she knew for certain what she has lost. If there's a force in the world that can make her whole, she doesn't yet know what it is. But again, she likes that he has asked.

She doesn't want to tell him what happened, though. It's too raw, this wound she can't identify. Instead she says, "The blood. It gives the gift of prophecy, doesn't it? Why so little?"

The smile he directs at the vial is sad. "Because knowledge of the future is an unchancy thing. We're caught between two blades at home—a war I don't want to join, but don't have any choice in. I need to know which side will keep my people safe, or at least as safe as they can be. But I would not want to reach any further than I must." Then he looks up at her. "If you wish, one drop of this is yours. I presume an archon who drinks of it will gain the gift, just as a mortal does. Or I will drink for you, and answer the question of your choice."

Before she paid the Lhian's price, she would have refused, out of the conviction that the future held nothing worth knowing. Now . . . now she refuses for a different reason. Ree shrugs and grins. "Eh. It takes away the excitement, knowing what will come next."

The Cruais accepts that rapidly enough that she knows the offer wasn't easy for him to make. Or maybe he can tell she's reveling in this moment of utter freedom: she can go anywhere from here, do anything at all. She's in no hurry to have someone, even a well-meaning prophet, push her down any particular path.

Ree introduces Aadet then, leaving him to explain how he got to the island, and what he went there for. It isn't her story to tell. The Cruais invites them to go back with him to his own territory; it's only a few days away by sea, and there, he promises, he will celebrate both their victories with a feast.

But Aadet, unlike Ree, has somewhere he needs to go. With many apologies, he says, "I should get back to my own people. They—they aren't exactly waiting for me, but—"

Ree takes him aside while the others pack up. "You got what you needed from the Lhian?" she asks quietly. He nods, and she says, "Then give it a few days to settle. Think through what you know, and how you're going to use it. A week more or less probably won't make any difference to the people of Solaike—but it might make a very big difference to what *you* do."

Aadet takes this in, eyes distant. She hasn't convinced him. Ree adds, "I'm pretty sure the Cruais's lands are close to a larger port—some place you can sail from. It may not take you straight home, but at least you'll be headed in the right direction."

He brightens and turns to tell the Cruais that he'd be delighted to accept the offer of hospitality. Ree, following, hides a grin. He doesn't need to know that she was lying through her teeth about the larger port. She has no idea where they are, much less the Cruais's own lands: that knowledge, if she ever had it, hasn't come back to her yet.

He'll find out eventually, of course. But she'll make it up to him. She's free, and she has a piece of her true name; she can go anywhere she likes. The more she thinks about it, the more she feels like starting with Aadet's own land.

After all, she hears there's going to be a revolution.

About the Author

MARIE BRENNAN is an anthropologist and folklorist who shamelessly pillages her academic fields for material. She is the author of several acclaimed fantasy novels including *A Natural History of Dragons*; The Onyx Court Series: *Midnight Never Come, In Ashes Lie, A Star Shall Fall,* and *With Fate Conspire; Warrior;* and *Witch.* Her short stories have appeared in more than a dozen print and online publications.

TOR·COM

Science fiction. Fantasy. The universe.

And related subjects.

*

More than just a publisher's website, *Tor.com*
is a venue for **original fiction, comics,** and
discussion of the entire field of SF and fantasy,
in all media and from all sources. Visit our site
today—and join the conversation yourself.